ANTON

ALL THE SINGLE DADS BOOK FIVE

SADIE KING

LET'S BE BESTIES!

A few times a month I send out an email with new releases, special deals and sneak peeks of what I'm working on. If you want to get on the list I'd love to meet you!

You'll even get a free short and steamy romance when you join.

Sign up here:
www.authorsadieking.com/free

ALL THE SINGLE DADS

These single dad hotties are fiercely protective and will do anything for the ones they love.

The series features grumpy single dads, secret billionaires, shy neighbors, and men turned obsessive by the curvy heroines who capture their hearts.

Each book in the series is a standalone but best enjoyed together. And look out for your favorite characters from Maple Springs popping in for cameo appearances.

All the Single Dads

Jaxon – Kali & Jaxon

Jake – Fiona & Jake

Levi – Aria & Levi

Brock – Olive & Brock

Anton – Eden & Anton

Xavier – Angela & Xavier

ANTON

ALL THE SINGLE DADS BOOK FIVE

He's a single father obsessed with the babysitter. But is she ready to give up her v-card for the single dad twice her age?

Anton

All the reasons why I shouldn't sleep with the babysitter:

She's half my age.

She's probably got a spotty boyfriend stashed away somewhere.

It would be weird for my kid, and I can't put him through anymore heartache.

The reasons I do sleep with the babysitter:

She was blowing on her soup in a really sexy way, and then she licked a strawberry.

I am so screwed.

Eden

Reasons why I shouldn't sleep with the silver fox single dad:

No. Can't think of a single one.

Reasons why I do sleep with the silver fox single dad:

He takes me on an all-expenses-paid trip to Chicago.

I drink too much wine.

He's damn hot and worth giving up my v-card for.

But now we're back home to reality, am I just his booty call?

EDEN

"*I*t's gonna crash!" Marcus smashes the toy car into the stack of books and the makeshift ramp falls to the floor with a heavy thump.

He leaps up excitedly. "I'm going to build it bigger this time."

I pick up a couple of the heavy books that have fallen just as the sound of his dad's raised voice comes from the other side of the living room door.

Marcus looks to the door, and I drop the books quickly, making a thumping sound.

"Do you think you can make the ramp go all the way from the table to the floor?"

The distraction works. His eight-year-old body, tall and slender for his age, spins to face me with an eager look on his face.

"From the dining table?" He assesses it carefully,

like I imagine his architect father assesses a model building.

His dad's angry voice comes from the other side of the door again and I jump up from the floor and move into the adjoining dining area.

"You'll need to make sure it's sturdy near the top here and the angle isn't too sharp."

My plan seems to work, and he moves with me into the dining area and further away from where his dad's having an angry phone conversation.

I help him bring the books through from the lounge and then close the dining room doors, so he's shielded from the phone call.

From the bits of the conversation I've heard, I'm sure it's Marcus's mom that his dad's talking too. And no kid needs to hear their parents arguing, even if they are divorced.

My phone buzzes in my pocket and I pull it out to see a message from my sister, Amy.

You free to chat?

I'm working

Babysitting isn't really working though. Stick the kid in front of the TV and give me a call. Isn't that what babysitters do?

I send an eyeroll emoji

Not this one

You've got too much integrity. You'll never make it in Vegas

Is that a compliment?

Of course not. You've got time to text, you've got time to chat

He hasn't even gone out yet

Is this the silver fox?

Prickly heat spreads up my neck and I glance quickly at Marcus. He's busy piling books up in stacks by the table, but I shield my phone anyway.

I regret the day I told Amy about my crush on Anton, the suave, no-nonsense dad of Marcus. He's about twice my age and there's no way he'd be interested in anyone as unsophisticated as me.

But that doesn't stop my heart racing every time he calls to ask if I can babysit.

Yes, it's the silver fox

Maybe he's not going out, he just wanted to see you

She sends a winking emoji

I don't think so, he's arguing with his ex-wife on the phone

Ow that's a lot of baggage. Why do silver foxes always come with ex-wives?

What do you know about silver foxes?

Nothing. Be careful

Careful of what? I'm just his babysitter. He doesn't even notice me

Then he's blind

I smile at my sister's words. She may tease me but underneath it all she's fiercely loyal and my biggest champion.

Thanks sis. Better go, Marcus is about to ruin the architect review collection

I don't know what that is. Call me when you can xx

"Marcus, use the national geographic magazines, not the architect ones."

I pull out a stack of old magazines from the bottom of the bookcase and take the thick and expensive looking architect ones off him. "Your dad won't be pleased if his magazines get ruined."

He grins at me. "You know him too well."

I smile awkwardly and take my position in the chair.

I do know him too well.

I know he loves basketball and plain polo necks and that he has a collection of sneakers that have barely been worn. I know he likes natural shaving products, he only uses grey towels, and he likes strong coffee beans from Ghana.

But I don't know how he drinks his coffee because everything I know about him is from nosing around his house once he's gone out and Marcus has gone to bed.

Yup, I'm slightly obsessed with Anton.

He's so much more sophisticated than any of the boys in this hick town, I mean he reads Architect Review for goodness sake. I don't know anyone in Maple Springs who reads anything other than car or fishing magazines.

But there's no way he'd be interested in a high school dropout like me, who's only good for babysitting and waitressing.

The sooner I get out of this town the better.

I bring up my banking app and check my balance: $378.77.

Enough to buy a bus ticket to Vegas but I need at least double that if I want to rent somewhere. A friend of mine can get me a waitressing job at the casino she works at and give me a bed for a couple of nights. But I need a little more money behind me before I make the move.

I slip my phone back in my pocket just as the dining room door bursts open.

Anton stands in the doorway, his broad frame almost taking up the whole space. His eyebrows are drawn together in a thunderous look that only accentuates his chiselled features. His blue eyes, made stormy by his mood sweep the room, taking in the stack of books, the pile of cars and his magazines being used as a car ramp.

His expression softens.

"Looks like a killer track, buddy."

5

Marcus grins widely at his father's praise. "I'm going to video it and put it online."

Anton frowns but he must have something bigger on his mind because his gaze snaps to mine.

My breath leaves my chest, and I can't breathe.

"Eden. Follow me."

My name on his lips sends a rush of heat through my body making me feel woozy. He turns and saunters out of the room, and on wobbly legs I get up and follow.

I follow him through the lounge and out to the hallway and he closes the door behind me.

He paces the front entryway, running a hand through his hair.

"What are you doing this Friday?"

My knees go weak. Could he, finally, be asking me out?

"Nothing." My words come out breathlessly. "I'm free."

Amy would say I'm being too available, that I should play hard to get. But the words are out before I can think.

"And the rest of the weekend?"

"I'm free all weekend."

"Good. We're going to Chicago."

I stare at him, and my mouth must be hanging open because he gives a short laugh.

"I've got an important client meeting and I need to

take Marcus with me, and I need you to look after him."

He's not asking me on a date. He's asking me to babysit.

I feel heat creeping up my neck. How could I be so stupid? Of course, this older, sophisticated man isn't asking me out. I'm just the babysitter.

"For the whole weekend?" My voice sounds meek as I try to regain my composure.

"I'll pay you, of course, as well as pay for the flights, hotel, meals and any expenses you need to keep Marcus entertained."

An all expenses trip away with the man I'm crushing on; this could be torture. But a whole weekend of working would just about get me the money I need for Vegas.

"Wendy was supposed to have Marcus, but she's booked a wine tour in California instead."

I like it that he refers to his ex by her name, not as his ex-wife. She's always Wendy, like he's trying to get away from any association with her.

"She knew I had this big meeting, but she claims she forgot. I must have reminded her ten times to make sure she wouldn't go flaky on me."

He runs his hands through his hair, and I can see his frustration. The single dad with custody, trying to have a successful career while raising a child on his own.

"It's okay, Anton." I place a reassuring hand on his shoulder. I've never touched him before and I'm surprised by the warmth from him. "I can be there; you don't have to worry about Marcus."

He looks down at my arm and then at me. His look is intense, and I don't know if it's the anger he still feels or something else.

When he speaks his voice is husky. "Thank you, Eden. If only all women were as reliable as you."

He puts his hand over mine and pats it before moving away.

I feel dismissed, like a father giving me a kind pat. Which of course he is old enough to be my father.

Then why do my legs feel wobbly whenever he's around?

2

ANTON

*T*he air hostess walks past, and I grab her attention.

"Do you want anything?" I ask Eden.

"Just a water."

"A water and another bourbon, please." The hostess nods and heads off to get our drinks.

If I'm going to keep my composure on this flight with Eden's thigh bumping against mine, then I'm going to need that bourbon.

Marcus insisted on having the window seat and he's snoring gently as we cruise 40,000 feet into the air. Which means that Eden is in the seat next to me.

I'm a big guy and with my substantial form spilling into my space, our thighs are bumping into each other. Her thin leggings against my jeans are causing friction that's driving me crazy.

She's reading a book, romance going by the couple

on the cover, completely unaware of the effect she's having on me.

And why would she be aware? She's got to be almost half my age. She probably thinks of me as more of a father than a lover. She's probably got a pimply boyfriend, or a smart college boy.

The hostess arrives with our drinks, and I take mine with trembling hands.

Eden sips her water slowly.

"Are you okay?"

She looks at me with genuine concern and I don't blame her. I'm sweating just sitting next to her.

I down my drink in one and let the warm liquid calm me.

"I didn't know you were a nervous flyer."

I let her think that's what's making me nervous, if she knew it's because I'm hiding a hard on under my food tray, she'd probably jump out of the plane.

"You been to Chicago before?"

She shakes her head. "Never left the state."

That surprises me. But then I remember she is only nineteen.

She puts her book down. "I want to go to Vegas."

Her eyes light up when she says it and I wonder what it would be like to take her there, to show her the city lights and flashy casinos.

"It's a great place to visit."

"I'm gonna live there one day."

I hope she's not serious. Vegas is no place for a

young woman. She sips her water nonchalantly and I decide it must just be a young girl's fancy. Everyone around here wants to go to Vegas.

"Thanks for coming on short notice. You're a life saver."

"It's a free trip to Chicago. I couldn't refuse."

"You got a boyfriend you had plans with?"

I don't realise I'm squeezing my plastic cup until it cracks.

She shakes her head, and my hand lets go of the squashed cup, feeling relief wash over me. I can't bear the thought of her being with anyone else.

"I'm not interested in any of the boys in Maple Springs."

"Good."

She looks surprised. "Boys are only after one thing," I add hastily.

I cringe at myself, now I'm lecturing her like I am her father.

She looks amused. "And how about men, what are they after?"

Her eyes sweep over me and at her gaze I feel my body come alive with heat. She bites her lip and lowers her lashes. Christ, she's flirting with me.

I lean in so I'm close to her, dropping my voice to a husky whisper.

"They're only after one thing too, but the difference is a man will know how to make you scream with pleasure."

Her breath hitches and her eyes go wide. She worries her lower lip, pulling at the skin.

This close I can see the pulse in her neck throbbing and if I kissed her now, I'm sure she'd let me.

"Can I take your empty cup?"

The hostess leans between us, breaking the moment.

I sit up straight in my chair handing over the broken cup. Eden picks up her book and the moment is lost.

I take a deep breath, trying to still my racing pulse.

"Another bourbon, please."

3

EDEN

*T*he wine glass is slippery in my sweaty fingers, and I take a big gulp to calm my nerves.

Across the table from me Anton is buttering a bread roll, looking calm and composed, at home in the hotel suite. Whereas I feel out of place and nervous as hell to be sitting across a dinner table from him, like we're equals.

"How's the Sancerre?"

I'm not sure what he's asking about, and he must see my confusion because his eyes twinkle in amusement. "The wine."

"Yeah, I knew that." I nod vigorously fooling nobody.

"It's good. It tastes like..." I take another gulp. I've got absolutely no idea how to talk about wine and

Anton must know it judging by his amused smile. "...it tastes like wine."

He chuckles and I relax a little.

"That's the best critique I've heard. But tell me, how do you like your soup?"

I had no idea what to choose from the room service menu, so Anton ordered for me. First course is a tomato and basil soup and it's steaming hot. I take a spoonful to my lips and blow on the hot soup before slipping it into my mouth.

The flavours zing on my tongue and I close my eyes as the heat warms my mouth.

"Mmm, that's good."

When I open my eyes, Anton's looking at me intensely, his body frozen. It's alarming, that look, but strangely exciting, like I'm the main course and he wants to eat me all up.

It makes me feel warm and wet between my legs and I look down feeling embarrassed.

I take another spoonful of soup and blow gently on it.

Anton makes a grunting noise, and I can't look at him because he's turning me on so much which is ridiculous because all he's doing is watching me eat soup.

In confusion I take another gulp of wine, finishing off my glass.

I don't have much experience with men. In fact, I don't have any experience with men, so I'm not sure if this dampness in my panties and strange pull I feel between my legs is normal.

To hide my awkwardness, I refill my wine glass and start talking.

I tell him all about the day I spent with Marcus. While Anton was seeing his client and visiting the proposed development site, I took Marcus to the zoo and then this cool interactive museum.

He was so tired he fell asleep on the couch as soon as we got back to the hotel. Anton transferred him to his bed and invited me to have dinner with him in their suite.

They're sharing a two-bedroom suite with a living area while I've got my own room across the hall.

Which is why we're here now, just the two of us, having a room service dinner while Marcus sleeps.

By the time we get to dessert, the bottle of wine is empty, and my head is feeling fuzzy. I stand up from the table and stumble.

Anton reaches out a hand to catch me and I sit back down abruptly, wondering where my ability to stand has gone.

"I think it might be time to get you to bed, Eden."

I giggle at his words. Is he going to take me to bed? But his look is serious.

He gets up from his seat and I lean on him as he lifts me out of my chair. His hand is on my arm, and he's so close it makes me feel woozy, in a good way. Like my knees are about to buckle.

This feeling I've had all night, this tug in my core, I can't ignore it any longer.

The wine makes me bold, and I reach up and run my fingers over the stubble on his chin and up his cheek until I'm cradling his face in my hand. His eyes go dark, and he takes my hand in his, gently moving it off his face.

"I think you've had too much wine."

He may be right, but his breathing is shallow, and his eyes hooded, and he has that look again like he wants to eat me all up for dessert.

I step toward him, going up on my tip toes to plant a kiss on his lips. He takes a sharp intake of breath and I move my lips over his again, softly kissing his mouth. My body leans into him, and like a brazen hussy, I press myself against him.

I gasp as I come up against something hard between his legs.

He's got a hard on and the knowledge makes my whole body tremble with desire. My knees go weak, and I push my hips against him.

He's breathing hard, like he's trying to resist me. Then I run my hands up his thigh and rub the hard lump in his jeans.

He groans, then his lips crash into mine. His hands grab my hips, and he grinds into me, his hard cock trying to impale me through the fabric of my leggings.

I'm gushing wetness between my legs and when his hand reaches there, my need is overwhelming. He pushes his palm against me, and through my leggings the friction is almost too much to bear.

There's the sound of a door opening, and we freeze.

"Dad?" Marcus's sleepy voice comes from the next room.

Anton steps back and I straighten up.

"We're in here."

I barely get my breathing under control before Marcus comes into the suite, rubbing his eyes sleepily.

"I'm hungry."

"I saved you some bread rolls."

Anton goes to the room service trays to sort the food for Marcus while I try to compose myself.

My heart is thumping so hard I'm sure I must be waking the whole hotel. My head is fuzzy from the wine and my body's hot and unsatisfied.

I kissed Anton, the silver fox. I threw myself at him until he kissed me back. I'm suddenly embarrassed and need to get out of here.

Grabbing my bag I head for the door. "I gotta go."

Anton starts to say something, but I pull open the door before he gets a chance and retreat across the hall to the safety of my own room.

4

ANTON

The next morning it's early when I knock on Eden's door. She's already dressed with hair wet from the shower. Her short skirt over leggings shows off the feminine curves of her wide hips. I lick my lips, thinking about the kiss we shared.

"I took advantage of you last night. I'm sorry."

She'd had too much to drink and even though I'd imagined that moment for weeks, it's not how it was meant to go. Not when her head was blurry from wine. It needs to be her choice, fully.

She pulls a strand of wet hair between her fingers.

"You didn't take advantage." Her eyes meet mine. "It's what I wanted."

My dick stirs at her words. I've wanted this woman since she first turned up to babysit. I didn't think she'd be interested in an old man like me. But here she is, proving me wrong.

Just then Marcus opens the door, searching for me.

"Can we order breakfast, Dad?"

I want to kiss Eden so bad, but I won't do that in front of my kid.

"Join us for breakfast?"

She nods and ten minutes later we're in the suite with a platter of fresh fruit and croissants.

"What are you two going to do today?"

Eden bites into a fresh strawberry and I try not to stare at the way her lips close around it, sucking it into her mouth.

"We're going to the pier today," says Eden between mouthfuls.

"Can you come with us, Dad? Please."

Marcus puts on his best pleading face until I pull up my phone and check my schedule.

"I have to meet some people this morning. But I can meet you after lunch."

I look at Eden when I say it and am pleased to see her face light up.

"I'll call you when I finish my meetings."

There's one client I'll have to cancel but I'm not missing the opportunity to spend the afternoon with Eden. I've had a taste of her and now I want more.

It's later that evening and I've just put Marcus to bed.

We spent the afternoon at Navy Pier, giddy from rides and too much cotton candy. Dinner was at a pizza place in town, the three of us sharing cheesy slices and sugary soda. Now finally, Marcus is in bed, and I have Eden all to myself.

She's waiting for me on the couch with her feet tucked underneath her as she reads her book.

I bring her a hot chocolate from the machine in the room. I'm not going to offer any alcohol tonight. I want to make her mine, and I want her to be fully aware when I do it.

She puts her book down as I hand her the steaming mug and I sit next to her.

"Thanks for today, for this weekend."

She shrugs. "That's what you pay me for."

"You're great with Marcus. He really likes you."

"He's a great kid."

He is. He's been my world since his mother left. The way she talks you'd think he was a lot of trouble, but he's not. He's no more trouble than any other kid.

She finishes her hot chocolate and I take the cup from her. She's looking at me expectantly and her eagerness makes me instantly hard.

I'm aware that Marcus is asleep in the next room, so I'm not taking any chances. I need to make this woman mine without interruption.

"Take a shower with me."

Her breath hitches and her breathing gets shallow.

"Together?"

The question is so innocent it goes straight to my heart.

I take her hand and lead her into my private en suite. We won't be interrupted in here.

"Yes, Eden, shower with me. I want to show you how a man takes care of his woman."

Her mouth pops open in surprise and her eyes go wide.

"I've got to tell you something."

My stomach sinks. This is where she tells me about the spotty boyfriend.

"I've never been with a man before."

She's looking down, her voice barely a whisper. I tilt her chin up so her eyes meet mine.

"What do you mean, honey? Are you a virgin?"

She nods, and her eyes dart away embarrassed. But this is the best news I've heard all day.

I run my hand up her thigh. "You mean to tell me that no one has touched this pussy?"

She nods. My hand runs over her panties, already damp with her need. "No one has put their cock in this little pussy?"

She whimpers and shakes her head. "No one."

My other hand cups her chin, and I bring my fingers down to pull at her full lips. The lips that have been driving me crazy all week.

My thumb holds her plump bottom lip down. "How about this mouth?" I slide my thumb between her teeth. "Has anyone put their cock in your mouth?"

She shakes her head, sucking gently on my thumb.

My cock goes rock hard. I want to be the first. The first cock to slide between those lips.

"Get ready, little girl, cause you're about to get fucked all kinds of ways."

5

EDEN

*a*nton has one hand between my legs and the other he pushes into my mouth. I suck on his thick thumb wondering what his cock tastes like.

He maneuvers me into the shower and turns the water on. I'm still fully clothed as he pushes me back against the bathroom wall, warm water spraying onto me.

The pressure increases between my legs and he's rubbing me in ways that make me feel like a live wire. Feelings I've never felt before spark from between my legs.

I moan but I can't speak because he's still got his thumb in my mouth.

"I'm going to make you come and then you're going to take care of me, little girl."

The words are so dirty and the pressure so intense

that I can only nod, wide eyed as he rubs between my legs.

Then his fingers slide into my panties and with one touch, I'm losing control. Vibrations emanate from the centre of my core. I gasp and moan and he must like that because his eyes are dark with desire.

"Good girl," he says as he slides his thumb out.

The water has made my clothes cling to me, and he pulls them off until I'm naked before him, the water from the shower on my back.

He kisses my lips and neck then he pushes the top of my head down. I know what he wants, and I sink to my knees.

His cock is sticking straight out, long and thick, making me gasp. I don't know how I'm going to get that huge thing in my mouth. He must sense my dilemma because he tilts my chin up so I'm looking at him.

"Start by licking it, just like you're licking an ice cream."

Taking the base of his cock in my hand I tentatively slide my tongue up his shaft. It tastes salty and sweet, and I lick it some more, widening my tongue to get all of his girth.

He leans back and moans.

"That's it, girl. Now pop it on your mouth like a strawberry."

He's watching me and with my eyes on him, I open my lips and slide the top of his dick between my teeth.

He groans, and spurred on by his pleasure, I suck gently, flicking my tongue as I do.

He growls. "You're a quick learner, little girl. Are you sure you've not had a dick in this mouth before?"

I shake my head and suck hard as I move my lips down his shaft.

"Jesus Christ."

I like making him moan and curse. I like this power that I have over him.

His hands slide round the back of my head, tangling in my hair. He pulls me toward him, forcing his cock into the back of my mouth. I gag and he lets up.

"You gotta open your throat, honey. Let me all the way in."

I relax my throat and this time when he thrusts, I'm ready.

His dick slides all the way to my tonsils, and he groans with pleasure. My hands reach for his balls and I caress them with my fingers.

He pulls my head up and down his cock, his eyes on me. "You're a good girl, letting me fuck your virgin mouth."

His words are so dirty, and as the thrusting gets more intense, my tits bounce up and down, slapping against the base of his cock.

"God, you're so sexy. I'm going to destroy this virgin mouth. Shoot my cum into you and claim it as my own."

The pull between my legs is increasing and as I

watch him getting off, I have an intense need I can't ignore. Spreading my thighs apart I reach my hand between my legs.

His eyes go wide as he watches me.

"Good girl." His voice is strained, and I know he must be close. "Get ready for my cum little girl."

I tug on his balls, and he tenses, then I feel hot liquid hit the back of my throat. At the same time I reach my peak, coming over my fingers. It's intense, the pleasure going all the way through my body.

I'm still trembling when he helps me to my feet.

"Did you swallow like a good girl?"

When I nod he smiles and wraps his arms around me. But I don't feel satisfied yet. I've had a taste of him and now I want it all.

I press my body against him and run my hands down to his manhood. I feel it growing hard under my touch.

"Can you go again?"

He chuckles. "Oh honey, for you, I can go all night."

6

ANTON

Two weeks later…

The sheet falls over the curves of her body and I run my hand over the rump of her ass. Even feeling her through the sheet makes my dick ache. Even though I've already had her twice this morning; once when she climbed on top of me, her eyes still half closed from sleep. And again, in the shower where she sunk to her knees like she did that first night a week ago and I took her virgin mouth.

Since that first time, her hunger for my cock seems insatiable. Last night after dinner, she crawled under the table and sucked me dry, her mouth still sticky with chocolate dessert.

She may have been a virgin two weeks ago, but now she's an experienced lover who can make me hard with one look.

Her eyes flutter open and she looks beautiful, looking up at me in the late morning light.

"Did I fall asleep?" she asks, sitting up on her elbows.

The sheet slips down her shoulder exposing one pert breast. The nipple is dark and instantly hardens under my gaze.

Her eyes follow my look, and she takes the nipple between her hand, rolling it lazily between her fingers as she looks me in the eye.

"Oh god," I moan as I climb back into bed.

It's a few hours later and we finally made it out of the bedroom.

The last two weeks have been heavenly. Eden's been around most nights. Once Marcus is in bed, she sneaks into the house, and we spend the nights making love. Then she's gone in the morning before he wakes up.

Marcus will be back from his mom's today, so I've packed Eden's bag for her and it's waiting by the door.

As I kiss her goodbye I feel a hesitation, like she wants to say something.

"What is it, honey?"

She looks at me nervously and bites her bottom lip. This weekend while Marcus is away at his mom's, Eden stayed all weekend. We've fucked so many times that my dick is sore.

But we've also made dinner together, talked,

picnicked in the garden, and made love on the picnic blanket under the stars.

Now she's looking at me like a lost little girl and I'm reminded of the age difference between us.

"I'm just wondering if you, um, want to hang out sometime?"

She looks at me expectantly but I'm not sure what she means.

"We've been hanging out all weekend."

"I mean, like, go out somewhere, together."

I lean back against the door frame. I get it now, she wants to date, like boys her age do.

Problem is, I'm not a boy, I'm a man. And I'm supposed to be her employer.

If she's seen around town with me, people will talk, and I don't want her being the centre of gossip. But most of all, I don't want it getting back to Marcus before I'm ready to tell him.

I cup her hand in my chin. Her skin is so smooth, so youthful.

"It's not a good idea right now, okay?"

She squints at me, disappointed.

"Soon, okay? I'll take you out soon."

She looks like she wants to say more but at that moment my phone rings. I give her a kiss on the forehead as I pull it out of my pocket.

I watch her walk down the drive clutching her bag. She doesn't look back and I have an uneasy feeling that I just said the wrong thing.

7

EDEN

"You're telling me he sneaks you into the house for sex, but he won't be seen out with you?"

Amy's looking at me incredulously. We're at Candy's Cafe a few days later and I'm spilling the beans about Anton. He had asked me to keep it quiet, but two weeks without telling my sister is pretty good.

"It's not like that," I say defensively. "We have to make sure Marcus doesn't find out."

"Find out his old man is taking advantage of the babysitter?"

"See. This is why we can't tell people."

She snorts. "Because they'll call him out."

I take a bite of my unicorn cookie and eye my sister. "This is why I didn't tell you; I knew you'd react like this."

"I'm just trying to look out for you, sis. You've never

had a boyfriend before, so you don't know this isn't normal boyfriend behaviour."

I chew my cookie slowly, wondering if she's right. The last two weeks have been the best of my life.

My body feels awakened and not only that, but I'm also more relaxed and less anxious than I've ever been. I like being with Anton, not only for what he does to my body, but he's kind and funny and easy to talk to.

"I think I might be in love with him."

Amy almost chokes on her coffee.

"Oh sweetie, this is bad."

"Why is it bad? Love is good, right?"

"Yeah, if it's both ways. But do you really think he loves you?"

There's a cold feeling in my heart and my stomach clenches. Amy's hand goes on my arm.

"Oh hon, I don't mean to upset you, it's just, it sounds to me he's only interested in sex. If he really liked you, he'd want to be seen with you. He'd take you out, show you off, he'd be finding a way to make it work. Not all this secretive stuff."

Maybe she's right. I have no experience with men. Maybe the things I've been feeling are only one way.

"What should I do?"

She looks pitifully at me.

"I'm not saying I'm right, because I might be wrong. But why don't you try saying no next time he booty calls you?"

"I'm not his booty call."

She raises her eyebrows at me. "How often does he call you?"

"Every few days."

"And what does he want when he calls?"

I think back to the last few conversations and my face falls. "He tells me to come over after nine. To come to the back door and text him when I'm there."

She's nodding. "Yup, definitely a booty call."

I slump in my chair. My heart feels heavy. There's half a unicorn cookie on my plate but I don't feel hungry. And I never not finish one of Bella's cookies.

Just then my phone rings and I glance at it sitting next to me on the table.

"It's him. What should I do?"

"If he asks you round tonight, tell him you're not available. If he wants to see you, ask him to meet you tomorrow for a drink or a walk or something. If he won't do it…"

She leaves the rest unsaid, but I know what she means. It's a test. A test to find out what I really mean to him.

"Hello." I answer the phone with trepidation.

"I've been thinking about you." My heart swells at his words, he must feel the same as I do. "Come round tonight."

I want to see him, but my eyes go to Amy and she's shaking her head and mouthing no.

"Um, I can't tonight. I'm helping Amy, um, dye her hair."

She gives me a WTF look.

"How about tomorrow? I need to see you."

His voice is deep and husky and there's heat between my legs just listening to him. But Amy is giving me a stern look, so I stand firm.

"Um, how about we go out somewhere instead?"

"Eden, I'm not ready for that yet."

My heart sinks. Amy's right. I am just a booty call. "Will you ever be ready, Anton?"

There's silence on the other end of the phone. "Don't rush me, Eden."

There's a warning note to his voice. But just because I'm young doesn't mean he can call all the shots.

"Sorry, Anton. But I'm not just your booty call."

There's stunned silence.

"Eden…"

"Goodbye Anton."

I hang up the phone with trembling fingers. Amy almost leaps out of her chair in excitement.

"Good for you! You did it!"

Then she sees my trembling lip and the tears threatening my eyes.

"Oh hon." She wraps me in a hug and as I cling to my sister I wonder if I've done the right thing.

8

ANTON

*I*t's two days later, two days since Eden said goodbye and hung up on me.

My first instinct was to go straight to her place to see her. But I need to give her some time. If she's decided she'd rather have a boy her age and not an old man with all the baggage, then I need to respect that.

"Dad." Marcus's sharp tone brings me back to the present. "You're spilling the milk."

I look down at the bowl of cereal with milk overflowing onto the kitchen counter.

"Shit." I put the carton down and grab a cloth. "And don't you repeat that word." I give Marcus a sharp look.

"Are you okay, Dad?"

I got rejected by a woman half my age. My body is missing the best sex I've ever had, and my heart is missing her warm smile, her silly laugh, and her conversation.

"I'm fine." I stretch my mouth into a smile, but Marcus doesn't buy it.

"Is it Eden, that you've been sneaking into the house?"

I pause with the cloth in my hand and stare at him. "You know about that?"

He shrugs. "I hear you wrestling sometimes."

Oh shit. "Wrestling?"

"Yeah, grunting and moaning and banging into the furniture."

I turn away to the sink and ring out the cloth so he can't see my expression. My son heard us having sex. I'm a terrible parent.

"Yeah, um, we like wrestling."

"Are you sad because she's not coming to wrestle anymore?"

He's got it in one. I miss the wrestling.

"Um, yeah." Man, parenting can be awkward sometimes.

"I like Eden, Dad. Aren't you seeing her anymore?"

He's looking at me with hopeful eyes. This kid's been through enough having his mother leave him. I don't want to give him false hope. He suddenly looks vulnerable, and I want to hold him close, pull him to me and protect him from all of life's hurts.

I crouch down so I'm eye level with him.

"I like Eden too. But it's complicated. I didn't want to let you know until I was sure it was serious."

"The wrestling sounds pretty serious."

Ah man, this kid's killing me.

"Why are you smiling, Dad?"

I ruffle his hair. "No reason, buddy. But let me get this clear, if I want to see Eden, if she wants to see me too, that would be okay with you?"

He looks confused. "Why wouldn't she want you, Dad?"

"I'm twice her age for a start."

He shrugs. "Stop wasting time, Dad. Go get her."

Ten minutes later, I leave Marcus in the car and ring Eden's doorbell. But it's her sister who opens the door. Her face drops when she sees me, and she folds her arms across her chest.

"If you're here for a booty call, you're too late."

I glance at Marcus waiting in the car hoping he didn't hear her; I don't have to explain what a booty call is.

"What do you mean too late? Where is she?"

The sister looks me up and down. "Why should I tell you?"

I admire her protection of her little sister; it makes me chuckle.

She squints at me. "What are your intentions toward my sister?

This is worse than meeting her father. But if the gateway to Eden is through her overprotective sister, then I'll play ball.

"I love her." The words surprise me as much as they do the sister.

Her mouth falls open. "Really?"

"Yes, really. I need to tell her and if she still wants to walk away then fine. But she needs to know."

"Oh shoot. You actually love her?"

I run my hands through my hair exasperated. "Can you just tell me where she is?"

"She's at the bus station."

"What? Why?"

The sister glances at her watch. "She's getting the bus to Vegas in twenty minutes. You better hurry!"

She calls the last words after me because I'm already racing to my car.

I jump in the driver's seat and hurtle through town. Marcus whoops as I run a red light.

"Don't ever try that," I tell him.

Then I'm at the bus depot, mounting the curb to get into the parking lot.

"Cool driving, Dad." He's got a massive grin on his face, but I've got no time to lecture him about safe driving. Feeling like a bad parent, again, I fling open the door.

"Stay here," I call as I jog across the tarmac.

There's a bus at one of the bays and a line of people waiting to board. Eden's at the end of the line and I breathe a sigh of relief.

"Eden!"

She turns at the sound of my voice, and I reach her, out of breath.

"What are you doing here?"

She looks happy to see me and sad all at once.

"Don't go to Vegas." I grab her hands in mine. "I love you, Eden. I want you to stay, to be in my life."

Her hands are warm in mine, but she hesitates and pulls them away. "Then why don't you want to be seen with me?"

"Oh honey, it's not like that. Things are complicated when you've got a kid. Marcus has been through enough. I had to be sure before I made our relationship public."

She doesn't look convinced, and I don't know what else I need to say to this woman.

"And how do I know you're sure now?"

I shake my head. She's not getting it. "Not me. I've always been sure. I have to be sure that you're sure."

"Me?" She looks confused.

"I'm twice your age, divorced and with an eight-year-old kid. It's a lot to take on, Eden. It won't be easy for you. I need you to be sure because once you're in our lives, I want you for good and I can't have another woman leave on Marcus."

I see it finally hit her; what getting involved with me means. She'll be an instant mom, and to a school age boy.

"Marcus lives with me full time; there's school runs and dinners and basketball games. You're not just starting a relationship with me; you're starting one with my son too."

She folds her arms across herself and bites her lip. I can see her processing and I hope to God she'll say yes.

It's torture waiting for her to speak, knowing my whole future happiness rests on her next words.

The bus conductor comes down the line and indicates her bag. "This going on?"

Eden hesitates. She looks to me and then past me to Marcus waiting in the car.

"No," she says to the conductor. "The bags aren't going. I'm not going."

Relief floods me. "Does that mean…?"

"Yes." She smiles. "Yes, I love you Anton and I love your smart, funny son as well. And if he's part of you, then I'm all in."

My arms go around her and my heart feels whole. I never thought I'd love again. I thought it would be me and Marcus going through life just the two of us. But I was wrong, I opened my heart to Eden, and I found love.

EPILOGUE

EDEN

Five years later...

"Join me in the shower."

Anton whispers the words in my ear as he brushes past me in the kitchen. Just loud enough so that I will hear, but not the children.

I watch him saunter through the kitchen in his sweatpants, with the t-shirt clinging to his back. He's just back from a jog, and the pungent scent of perspiration follows him and makes my body tingle in anticipation.

I'm in the third trimester of my second pregnancy and horny as hell. And he knows it too.

I swing Fin out of the highchair and put him on the play mat.

"Marcus, can you watch your brother for a half hour? I just need to do a few chores upstairs."

Marcus holds his hands out and his brother toddles into them a wide grin on his face.

"Hey buddy, should we hang out for a bit?"

Fin giggles. He loves his older brother. "Trains, trains."

"Should we play trains?"

I leave them piecing together the wooden train set and head for the door.

"Mom," Marcus calls after me and I turn in the doorway. "You're coming to the game tonight, right?"

His basketball team has made it to the state final and the big game is tonight.

"I wouldn't miss it. Aunty Amy is going to babysit Fin, so we'll be there."

He grins. "Good."

I leave them to it and head up the stairs.

Anton's already got the shower running when I reach the bathroom. He's lathering his body with soap, and I watch him hungrily as I peel off my clothes.

Without a word, I step into the shower and sink to my knees.

WHAT TO READ NEXT

ALL THE SCARS WE CANNOT SEE

Man is not meant to live alone. He becomes dangerous, possessive, protective of what's his. And she is all mine...

Since retiring from the military, I don't like human company.

Until I meet Emily, my new neighbor.

She's as damaged as I am and running from her own demons.

When they catch up with her, I must fight my own inner darkness to protect the woman I love.

But two broken hearts don't always make a whole...

All the Scars We Cannot See is an instalove mountain man romance featuring a scarred ex-military recluse and the curvy girl on the run who steals his heart.

Keep reading for an exclusive excerpt or visit:
mybook.to/AllTheScarsWeCannotSee

ALL THE SCARS WE CANNOT SEE

CHAPTER ONE

Sam

Dust kicks up from the gravel and swirls around the car as it makes its way along the access road. Burgundy red Corolla. Early model hatchback with a dent in the passenger side door and one side mirror hanging off. It's barely roadworthy and certainly not the kind of vehicle suitable for the roads this far up the mountain.

Picking up my binoculars, I try to make out the driver. Through the dust haze, I can tell they're a woman with long dark hair and wearing wide sunglasses.

Probably a lost tourist out looking for an adventure off the beaten track. Only the back seat is loaded with belongings, making the back end of the car sag under the weight.

She must be lost. There's only my place and the

abandoned farm up this road. It's the reason I bought this cabin. No neighbors. No tourists. Just me and the mountain.

Until this beat-up little car turned up on my access road.

I guess she'll figure out soon enough that this road doesn't lead anywhere. Then she'll turn around and go home.

Even as I'm thinking it, the car starts to slow down. It turns into the driveway to the abandoned farm. She'll turn around there and head back the way she came, back to the tourist trails where she belongs.

Only she doesn't. The car turns all the way into the driveway and stops just outside the farmhouse.

The driver's door opens, and a pair of long, thick legs step out. I adjust the focus on the binoculars to take her in.

She's got her back to me, giving a good view of her curvy hourglass figure, wide hips encased in ass-hugging leggings, and long dark hair hanging over her shoulders.

My blood rushes to my dick, and it's suddenly hard to breathe.

"Damn."

I pull the binoculars off my eyes and turn my head away, trying to get my racing pulse under control. It's been a long time since a woman had that kind of effect on me. Not that I get the chance to see many women these days.

Running a hand through my hair, I take a swig of the cool beer sitting next to me on the coffee table.

It does nothing to quench my thirst.

As soon as I raise the binoculars and train them on the woman, my throat goes bone dry.

Her hips sway as she walks to the front door of the house. That old farm has been empty since I moved in three years ago, so if she's expecting to call on someone, she'll be disappointed.

But she doesn't ring the bell. Instead she reaches for her keys and jiggles the lock. A moment later, she pushes open the front door and disappears into the house.

"Damn," I mutter for the second time as I lower the binoculars.

Looks like I got myself a new neighbor.

To keep reading visit:
mybook.to/AllTheScarsWeCannotSee

GET YOUR FREE BOOK

Sign up to the Sadie King mailing list for a FREE book!

You'll be the first to hear about exclusive offers, bonus content and all the news from Sadie King.

To claim your free book visit:
www.authorsadieking.com/free

BOOKS BY SADIE KING

Maple Springs

Small Town Sisters

Candy's Café

All the Single Dads

Men of Maple Mountain

Wild Heart Mountain

Wild Heart Mountain: Military Heroes

Wild Heart Mountain: Wild Riders MC

Sunset Coast

Underground Crows MC

Sunset Security

Men of the Sea

The Thief's Lover

The Henchman's Obsession

The Hitman's Redemption

For a full list of titles check out the Sadie King website

www.authorsadieking.com

ABOUT THE AUTHOR

Sadie King is a USA Today Best Selling Author of short instalove romance.

She lives in New Zealand with her ex-military husband and raucous young son.

When she's not writing she loves catching waves with her son, running along the beach, and good wine, preferably drunk with a book in hand.

Keep in touch when you sign up for her newsletter. You'll even snag yourself a free short romance!

www.authorsadieking.com/free

FOLLOW ME ON BOOKBUB

Follow Sadie King on BookBub to get an alert whenever she has a new release, preorder, or discount!

www.bookbub.com/authors/sadie-king

Milton Keynes UK
Ingram Content Group UK Ltd.
UKHW011822170823
427026UK00001B/37